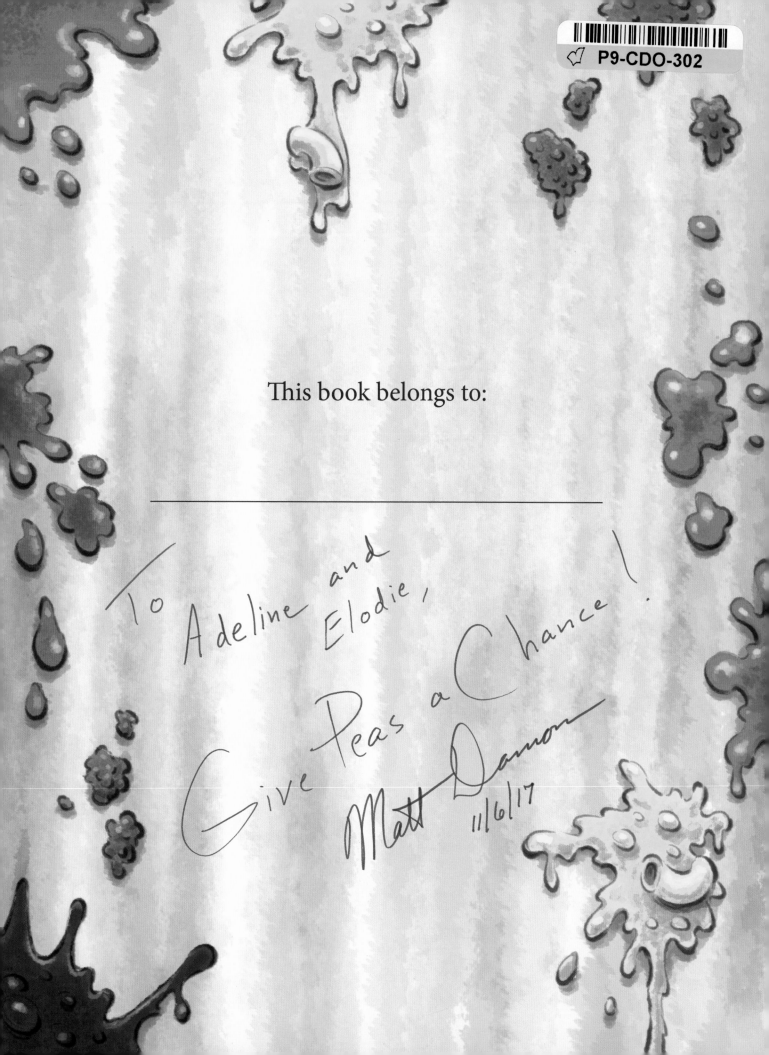

This book belongs to:

_____

To Adeline and Elodie,
Give Peas a Chance!
Matt Damon 11/6/17

To Jennie, Hana and Maile.
With love and affection.
The mantra is always "yum."
–M. D.

I dedicate the pictures in this book to my son, Milo.
Long may you munch!
–G. K.

Life in the Fridge was quite peaceful and cool,
While under Queen Honeydew's virtuous rule.
The Queen led with fairness and never was cruel,
To the richest desserts nor the poorest, thin gruel.

The food groups were blessed by her wisdom and grace,
And each sort of food had its own proper place.
The fruits claimed the top shelf as their special space.
The next section down was the vegetable base.

The middle shelf held an odd mixture of stuff,
Like pastas and cheeses and small pastry puffs.
Below them were meats, who seemed rowdy and rough,
Though deep down inside they were tender, not tough.

On the bottom shelf sat the desserts and the treats,
Who were mostly well known to be kind, gentle sweets.
Each shelf was well kept. Each was tidy and neat,
With all foods well sheltered from dryness and heat.

One summer morning, the door opened wide.
A new jar of cherries was welcomed inside.
"Come live on *our* shelf," the friendly fruits cried.
So, the cherries were placed by the olive jar's side.

When a cherry named Rosaline came out to play,
An olive named Romeo shouted, "Hooray!"
They bounced with each other and then rolled away,
To play hide-and-seek on the fruit salad tray.

"Romeo Olive, you're playful and fast.
But why are you salty?" the sweet cherry asked.
"I'm stored in a brine," he said. "So I'll last.
But like you I grew on a tree in the past."

Well, it was a wonderful, welcome surprise,
When both of these fruits, with their very own eyes,
Saw they'd made a friend of the same shape and size.
But then they heard shouting and loud, angry cries.

A leftover custard was making a fuss,
Wielding his sword, making threatening thrusts.
"I'm General Custard the Infamous,
And I say the cherries belong down with us.

"Sweet maraschinos, I think you should know,
Belong on desserts for good taste and good show.
So, Queen, I demand that you send them below.
And if you do not, I'll declare you my foe."

This grumpy old custard was mighty upset.
These cherries were foods he was greedy to get.
If on top of his filling sweet cherries were set,
He was sure to be known as the best dessert yet.

The Queen then replied from her high, royal seat,
"Old Custard you're different from most other treats.
Perhaps you were cooked at an unwholesome heat.
It seems that your filling is bitter, not sweet.

"Maraschinos are sweets. That is partially true.
But truth can depend on a food's point of view.
Now, I say the cherries may choose what they do.
Since they say they're fruit, I declare they are too."

Old Custard fell silent, then slipped out of sight.
But he spoke to the sweets on that very same night,
"The Queen isn't fair and she doesn't rule right.
We sweets have been cheated and now we should fight.

"We must stop this problem right down at its roots,
Or there'll be a day when all sweets are called fruits.
Let's thump that ripe melon and give her the boot.
Then I'll be the king all the foods must salute."

Up to the meats Custard shouted his speech,
"The next thing you know, the Queen's wisdom will teach
That a sausage is squash and a burger a peach!
Come fight with me meats, I do beg and beseech!"

The meats were all swayed by his strong point of view.
They cried out, "A food fight is long overdue!"
The sweets, they agreed, "It is true. It is true.
We will not be ruled by that dumb honeydew!"

A baloney brigade, with a pie and a prawn,
Snuck up to the fruit section just before dawn.
They foodnapped the cherries with boldness and brawn.
When other fruits woke, the poor cherries were gone.

The Queen wasn't one to use soldiers and troops,
She preferred to have peace among all the food groups.
But that day she declared, "I must whoop my war whoop,
For the cherries are foodnapped by vile nincompoops."

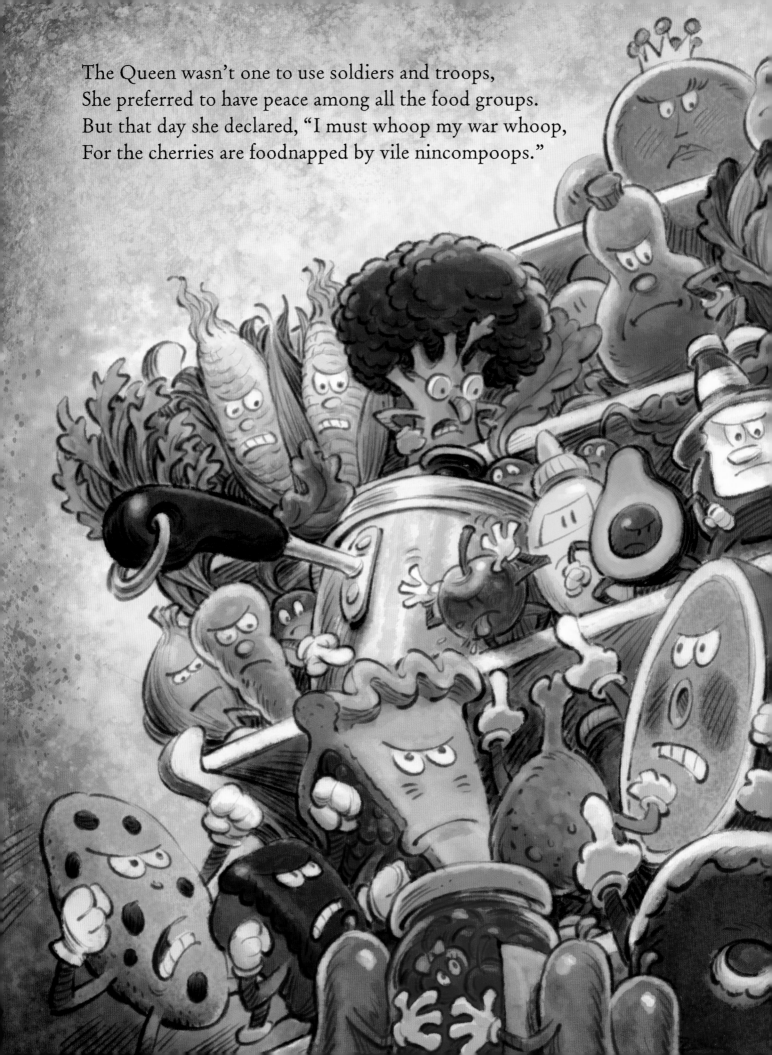

A war was declared, so the foods did divide.
The sweets and the meats were on Old Custard's side.
While most other foods let the Queen be their guide,
Some terrified turnips decided to hide.

Now, Romeo Olive, that round, shiny lad,
Was a little bit scared, but mostly just mad.
He thought to himself, *Oh, egad, this is bad.*
Food fights are awful and wasteful and sad.

He knew that most foods were quite decent and kind,
But ever since Custard got war on their minds,
The peace in the Fridge had begun to unwind.
Was Rosaline safe? It was her he must find.

So Romeo rolled off to find her in haste.
He rolled despite fear of the dangers he faced.
He hadn't one minute to worry or waste.
The start of the war he could practically taste.

It was Custard's fierce forces that fired food first.
A fat fudge-sauce bomb landed loudly and burst.
Three beets were bruised badly and had to be nursed.
Some pies charged in hard with a large liverwurst.

Salamis and sausages, made in New York,
Tossed the fresh salad with help from the pork.
The sweet, bubbly wine shot her dangerous cork.
And chocolate bonbons were launched from a fork

Once Custard's food army began its attack,
The Queen's cuisine was then forced to fight back.
The mustard yelled, "Custard's a big, brainless snack!"
And a cabbage rolled over the liverwurst's back.

All the fruits and the vegetables lined up in rows.
On the Queen's first command they charged at their foes.
A platoon of potatoes, from East Idaho,
Attacked the lime jello with balls of bread dough.

As Romeo rolled down the bombed battlefield,
He hadn't one weapon of war he could wield.
He had no thick armor, no helmet, no shield.
He almost got fudged and then nearly oatmealed.

He dodged the two armies and rolled very far,
Without getting bumped or bruised or scarred.
But as he rolled nearer to Rosaline's jar,
He was spied by Old Custard, who watched from afar.

Young Romeo's search for the cherries it seemed
Had gotten Old Custard most mightily steamed.
The General pointed his sword and then screamed,
"I command that that olive be peeled and then creamed!"

Now Romeo's fate looked much worse than just grim,
As the meats and the sweets were gathered 'round him.
The chance for escape was far slimmer than slim,
Then Rosaline leapt from the cherry jar's rim.

When she landed, she shouted so all foods could hear,
"Beside this brave olive I'll stand firm and near!
I'm a sweet and a fruit. That is perfectly clear.
There's no reason why innocent foods should be smeared.

"We food groups have different shapes and tastes,
And now fears in our hearts, which Old Custard has placed.
But look—we're all foods, and the fact must be faced,
That mashing each other is simply a waste.

"We must all refuse to take part in his game.
Should foods fight a war so that Custard finds fame?
Well, I say, 'No way!' And I'm willing to claim,
That other fine foods of the Fridge feel the same."

The meats and the sweets they all suddenly froze,
For foods respect courage, most everyone knows.
Then, meanwhile, the olives and cherries each chose
To line up at Romeo's side in tight rows.

A meatball, whose name was Sir Roland O'Dew,
Called out to his friends in the thick, meatball stew,
"Let's join these bold olives and brave cherries too.
Let's join in this peace plan, this wise switcheroo."

So, out of their pot, meatballs hopped one by one,
Till inside the pot was a total of none.
Some peaceful green peas joined what had begun.
The sesame seeds jumped right off their bun.

The small, baby wieners and eggs scrambled out,
With sausages, beans and some shy sauerkraut.
A frosted fudge brownie gave a hug to a sprout.
"That Rosaline's right," wrinkled raisins did shout.

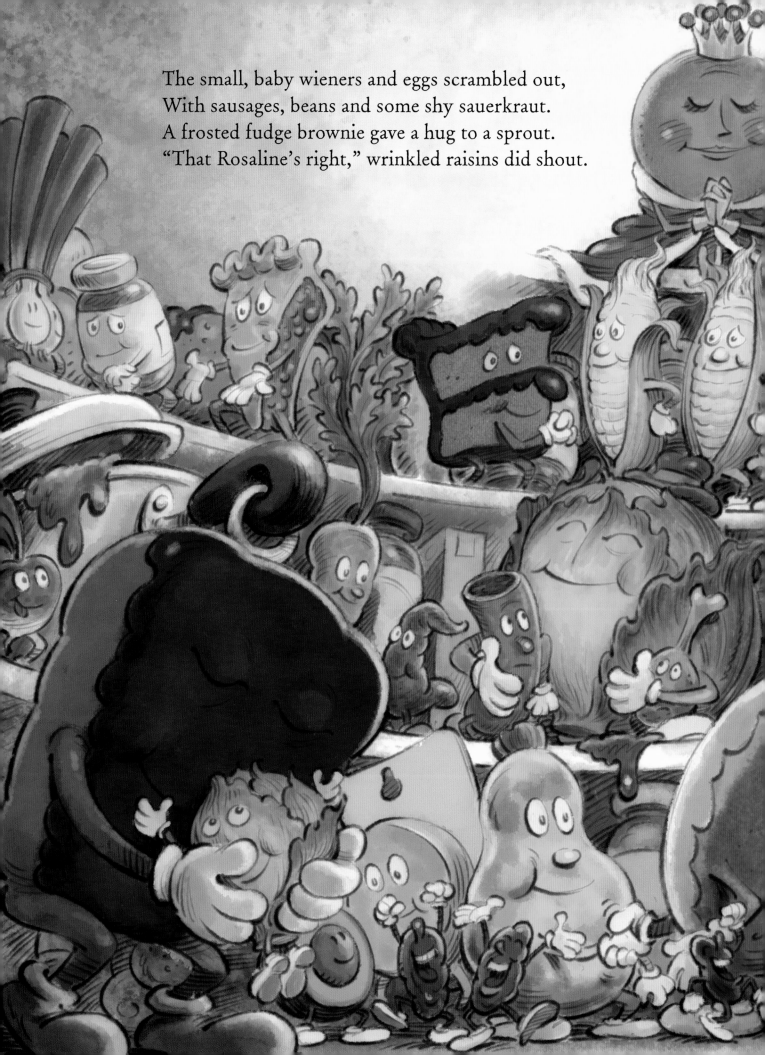